Sick Day

by Steven Banks   illustrated by Barry Goldberg

Simon Spotlight/Nickelodeon
New York London Toronto Sydney Singapore

 SIMON SPOTLIGHT

An imprint of Simon & Schuster Children's Publishing Division
1230 Avenue of the Americas, New York, New York 10020

SIMON SPOTLIGHT and colophon are registered trademarks of Simon & Schuster.
Manufactured in the United States of America
First Edition 10 9 8 7 6 5 4 3 2 1
ISBN 0-689-85848-5

One day after school Jimmy Neutron showed everyone his latest invention.

"Jimmy, this is your greatest ever!" shouted Sheen.

"I have to admit the Neutronic Sick Patch *is* amazing. Put it on and you look sick, take it off and you're okay. It's the best way to get out of school!" he said.

"Yay!" all his friends cheered.

The next morning all the kids put on the patches and became sick. But later when they tried to take them off, the patches had dissolved into their skin!

Their parents tried everything to get them well.

Carl's dad put him in a plastic bubble.

Cindy's mother stuck her with acupuncture needles.

Sheen's father gave him the pepper treatment.

Libby's mother tried an old-fashioned cure with a wasp sting.

And Jimmy's dad made him drink a disgusting homemade health shake!

Cindy and Libby called Jimmy for help.

"Neutron," said Cindy, "you'd better get us well or you're in big trouble!"

"Our parents are driving us crazy!" complained Libby.

"I can fix that," Jimmy said, and called Carl and Sheen. "Meet me at the lab as fast as you can," he cried.

Jimmy told Carl and Sheen his idea. "I'll have to shrink to microbe size, go inside one of you, and get the sick germ so I can cure us all with a vaccine," he explained.

Sheen raised Carl's hand. "I volunteer Carl to be the one we go inside!"

"I accept—hey! Wait a minute!" said Carl.

"Goddard, commence shrinkage!"
commanded Jimmy.
Goddard aimed the shrink ray at
Jimmy, Sheen, and the hover car.

ZAP!

"So begins our journey to the center of Carl," said Jimmy.
"Full speed ahead!" shouted Sheen.
Jimmy steered the hover car into Carl's nose.
"Be careful in there!" cried Carl.

"Hey, Carl? When was the last time you cleaned in here?" asked Sheen.
Carl twitched his nose as the hover car rode through it.

Jimmy grabbed his communicator. "Carl! Do not sneeze! I repeat, do not
sneeze! You could blow us to kingdom come!"

Carl pinched his nose with his fingers. "I'll try not to!" he said.

"Look, Sheen! There's Carl's brain!" said Jimmy.
Sheen looked around. "Where? Is it behind that teeny, tiny rock?"
Jimmy shook his head. "Uh . . . no. It *is* that teeny, tiny rock."
"Wow!" said Sheen. "It's bigger than I thought it would be!"

Sheen stood up excitedly. "Hey, Jimmy! There's that thing people always punch in cartoons! I'm gonna take a whack at it!"

"Don't do it!" warned Jimmy. "That's Carl's uvula. If you touch it, you could make Carl throw us up!"

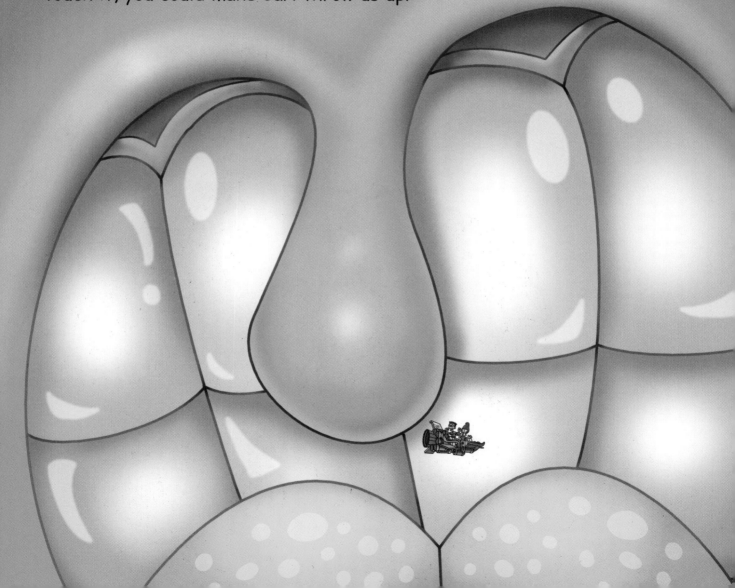

Suddenly the hover car dropped down Carl's throat!
"Hold on, Sheen!" yelled Jimmy. "It's gonna be a bumpy ride!"

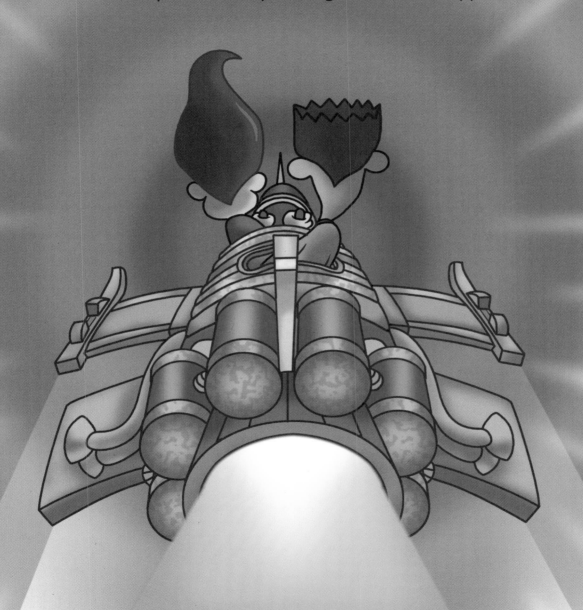

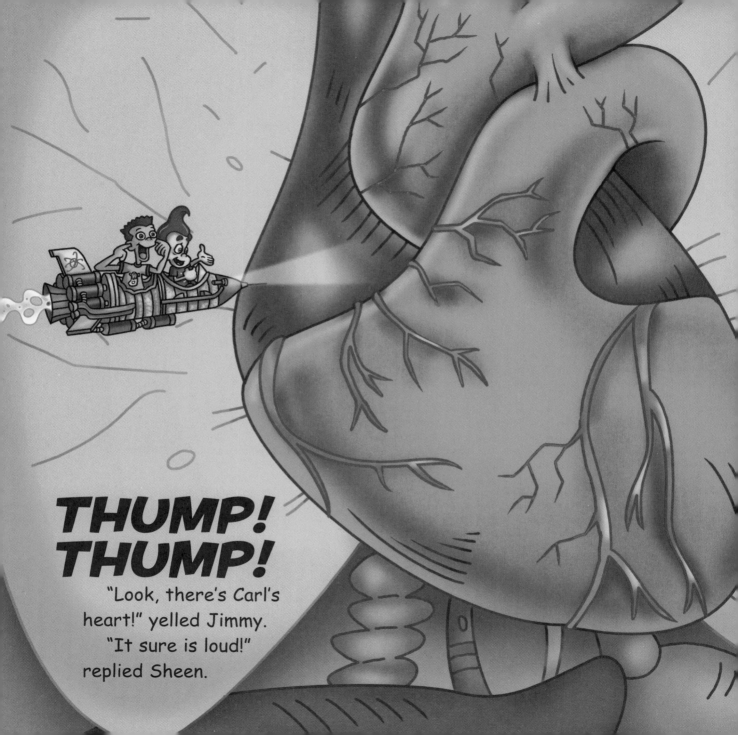

THUMP! THUMP!

"Look, there's Carl's heart!" yelled Jimmy. "It sure is loud!" replied Sheen.

SPLASH!

"We've reached our destination," announced Jimmy. "Carl's stomach."

Sheen shook his head. "Man, Carl sure eats a lot of junk!"

"Never mind that," said Jimmy. "We've got to find a germ for the cure!"

Jimmy pulled out his Neutroscope and began to search. "There's one!" cried Jimmy, pointing to a little green object floating by. "I just need to catch it."

When Jimmy grabbed the germ, it made a funny noise.
Jimmy turned around and saw hundreds of germs racing toward him.
"Pukin' Pluto! We're under attack!" he yelled.

"Sheen, get the germs' attention! Do something!" cried Jimmy.
"But what should I do?" asked Sheen. "Sing? Dance? Tell jokes?"
"Do it all!" shouted Jimmy. "Just get 'em away from me!"
Sheen began to sing and dance and make jokes, but none of the germs paid any attention to him.

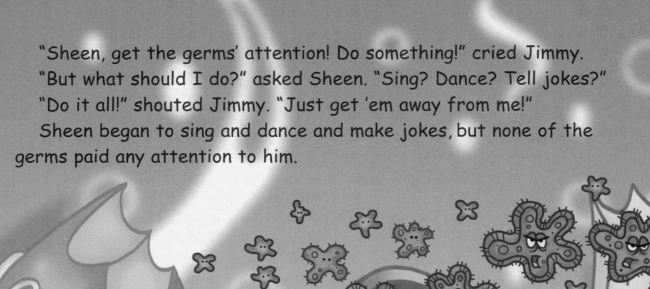

"Think! Think!" said Jimmy. "Brain blast!"

Jimmy remembered that germs were attracted to saltwater. "Tears have salt in them! Sheen, start crying!"

"But I'm not sad!" Sheen said, protesting.

"Pretend that the *Ultra Lord* show isn't on TV anymore!" yelled Jimmy.

"Waaah!" Sheen cried, and all the germs rushed over to him.

Jimmy jumped into the hover car. "I've got the germ! Now let's get out of here fast!"

They raced back up Carl's throat but the germs were trailing them!

"Let's make Carl sneeze," said Jimmy. "That'll get us out!"

"I've got some pepper left over from when my dad tried to cure me!" said Sheen.

Sheen shook some pepper into Carl's nose, and he let out a huge sneeze.

"AH-CHOO!"

The next day Jimmy cured everyone, and they all returned to school.
"I can't believe I'm saying this, but I'm actually glad to be here!" said Jimmy.
Everyone agreed.

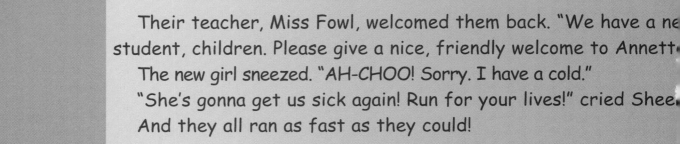

Their teacher, Miss Fowl, welcomed them back. "We have a ne
student, children. Please give a nice, friendly welcome to Annett
The new girl sneezed. "AH-CHOO! Sorry. I have a cold."
"She's gonna get us sick again! Run for your lives!" cried Shee
And they all ran as fast as they could!